❥❧ Mary Engelbreit's ❧❥
"Sweetie Pie"

Mary Engelbreit's
"Sweetie Pie"

Art copyright © Mary Engelbreit Ink, 1993
is a registered trademark of
Mary Engelbreit Enterprises, Inc.

Edited by Jill Wolf
Text copyright © 1993
Antioch Publishing Company
ISBN 0-89954-312-X

Printed in the U.S.A.

Note: Some measurements in parentheses
are British Imperial measure.

AN ANTIOCH GOURMET GIFT BOOK

✿ Mary Engelbreit's ✿

SWEETIE PIE

Art by Mary Engelbreit
Edited by Jill Wolf

Antioch Publishing Company
Yellow Springs, Ohio 45387

Nothing is sweeter than love . . .
　　　　　　—*Thomas à Kempis*

❧ CONTENTS ☙

Raspberry Hearts

$^1/_2$ lb. softened butter
$^3/_4$ cup (6 fl. oz.)
    granulated sugar
1 large egg
grated peel of 1 lemon

2 $^1/_2$ cups (20 fl. oz.)
    unbleached flour
pinch of salt
raspberry preserves
    (at room temperature)
confectioners' (icing) sugar

Mix thoroughly the butter, granulated sugar, egg, and lemon peel. Cut in flour and salt. Mix dough well, form a ball, and knead. Wrap dough in waxed paper; chill for 2 to 3 hours. Divide dough into halves. On lightly floured, cloth-covered board, roll out one half to $^1/_8$-inch thickness; repeat with other half, but roll quickly and keep dough chilled. From one half cut out solid heart shapes with cookie cutter; from other half cut out heart shapes, but also cut a small hole in the center of each shape. Prick all hearts with fork. Heat oven to 375° F. Butter cookie sheets lightly. (Always use a cold, clean, rebuttered sheet for each batch.) Bake in center of oven for 8 to 10 minutes or until golden. Immediately remove from sheet; cool on wire rack. Spread preserves on solid cookies. Cover with cookies with center holes. Dust with confectioners' sugar. Fill in center with more preserves.

— — — — — — — — — — — — — — — —

It is only with the heart that one can see rightly; what is essential is invisible to the eye. —Antoine de Saint-Exupery

9

Chocolate Chip Kisses

5 large egg whites
1 cup (8 fl. oz.) extra fine sugar
¹/₂ cup (4 fl. oz.) chocolate chips

Heat oven to 250° F. Line cookie sheets with oiled
brown paper. In a large mixing bowl beat egg whites
with an electric mixer on high speed for 5 minutes
until stiff, but not dry. Sprinkle ¹/₄ cup (2 fl. oz.) of
the sugar over the egg whites. Beat 3 more minutes.
A tablespoon at a time, sprinkle the remaining sugar
over the egg whites, folding in gently but thoroughly
with a rubber spatula. Very gently fold in chocolate
chips. Drop mixture by heaping tablespoons onto the
lined cookie sheets. Bake for 55 minutes. Remove
from oven. Immediately transfer cookies to wire
racks to cool, preferably in a warm and draft-free
area.

Tip: Make meringue cookies on a clear, dry day since egg whites
tend not to stiffen when it is humid.

All love is sweet,
Given or returned.
—Percy Bysshe Shelley

Orange Zabaglione

6 egg yolks (at room temperature)
2 tsp. (1 ¹/₂ Br. tsp.) sugar
1 cup (8 fl. oz.) fresh orange juice
¹/₂ tsp. almond extract
1 tbsp. (³/₄ Br. tbsp.) finely grated orange peel

Place yolks in top of double boiler. Add sugar; beat with a wire whisk, rotary beater, or portable mixer until mixture is thick and lemon-colored. Put top of double boiler over hot water. Add orange juice gradually, beating constantly. Add almond extract. Beat until zabaglione is the consistency of thick cream. Remove from heat. Spoon into sherbet glasses. Sprinkle with orange peel. Serve hot or chilled.

Always I have a chair for you
in the smallest parlor in the world,
to wit, my heart.

—Emily Dickinson

SWEETEST

HEART

ME

Strawberry Delights

Strawberries in Wine

1 pint fresh strawberries, cut in half
3 tbsp. (2 1/4 Br. tbsp.) sugar
1/2 cup (4 fl. oz.) white wine, champagne, or ginger ale

Place strawberries in glass container with lid.
Sprinkle with sugar and stir gently. Pour wine over
strawberries. Cover and chill in refrigerator at least
60 minutes. Serve in dessert glasses.

Strawberries with Dip

Wash and drain large whole berries, keeping stems on
them. Let dry. Combine dip ingredients; stir until
smooth. Place berries and the dip in serving bowls.

Plain Dip:
2 cups (16 fl. oz.) sour cream + 6 tbsp. (4 1/2 Br. tbsp.)
confectioners' (icing) sugar

Chocolate Dip:
Add 2 tsp. (1 1/2 Br. tsp.) vanilla extract and 4 tsp.
(3 Br. tsp.) Dutch cocoa powder to plain dip.

Sweets to the sweet . . .
—William Shakespeare

Chocolate Crêpes

2 tbsp. (1 1/2 Br. tbsp.)
   cocoa powder
1 cup (8 fl. oz.) sifted all-
   purpose flour
1/4 cup (2 fl. oz.) sugar
1/4 tsp. salt
3 eggs
1 cup (8 fl. oz.) milk

1/2 tsp. vanilla
2 tbsp. (1 1/2 Br. tbsp.)
   melted butter
butter for brushing pan
confectioners' (icing) sugar
vanilla ice cream or
   sweetened whipped cream

Sift dry ingredients into a medium-sized mixing bowl. In another bowl beat the eggs with an electric mixer for 5 minutes at medium speed or until thick. Stir the milk, vanilla, and butter into the eggs, then blend egg mixture into flour mixture until smooth. Place a large piece of waxed paper on a clean surface. Lightly brush an 8-inch crêpe or omelette pan with butter. Put pan on medium heat until butter bubbles. Pour in a scant 1/4 cup (2 fl. oz.) batter. Quickly swirl so batter covers bottom of pan. Cook until set, then loosen crêpe with spatula. Gently lift; turn to other side. Cook for a few seconds. Remove from heat; carefully loosen crêpe and slide onto waxed paper. Cook crêpes until batter is gone. Fold crêpes into quarters. Dust with confectioners' sugar. Top with vanilla ice cream or sweetened whipped cream.

Love is best. —Robert Browning

Peach Sorbet

3/4 cup (6 fl. oz.) sugar
1/4 cup (2 fl. oz.) light corn syrup
1 cup (8 fl. oz.) water
8 fresh, ripe, medium-sized peaches
2 tsp. (1 1/2 Br. tsp.) lemon juice

Combine sugar, water, and corn syrup in a small
saucepan. Bring to a boil over medium heat. Cool to
room temperature. Peel peaches, remove pits, and
dice peaches into a large bowl. Toss with lemon juice
to coat. Purée half of peaches in a blender or food
processor. Process other half. Stir peach mixture into
cooled syrup. Pour into the canister of an ice cream
maker and freeze according to manufacturer's
directions. If you do not have an ice cream maker,
freeze in a 9-inch square pan covered with foil for 3
to 6 hours or until firm. Break into pieces, then beat
with an electric mixer in a chilled bowl until light
and fluffy. Refreeze for about 3 hours and serve.

If we are truly prudent
we shall cherish those noblest and
happiest of our tendencies
—to love and to confide.
—Edward Bulwer-Lytton

Brownie Cupcakes

4 ounces semisweet chocolate
$^1/_2$ lb. butter
4 eggs
1 tsp. ($^3/_4$ Br. tsp.) vanilla extract
1 cup (8 fl. oz.) flour
1 $^3/_4$ cups (14 fl. oz.) sugar
1 cup (8 fl. oz.) chopped walnuts

Heat oven to 325° F. Melt chocolate and butter over
very low heat. Remove from heat. Add eggs and beat.
Add remaining ingredients, mixing until blended.
Place paper baking cups in standard-size muffin tin.
Pour batter into baking cups, filling about two-thirds
full. Bake for 35 minutes.

Isn't it delicious
To be a birthday child?
—Rose Fyleman

17

Ice Cream Cake

4 eggs, separated
$^1/_3$ cup (2 $^2/_3$ fl. oz.) sugar
$^1/_2$ tsp. vanilla extract
$^1/_2$ cup (4 fl. oz.) sugar
$^2/_3$ cup (5 1/3 fl. oz.) cake
   flour
$^1/_4$ cup (2 fl. oz.) cocoa
   powder

1 tsp. ($^3/_4$ Br. tsp.) baking
   powder
$^1/_4$ tsp. salt
sifted confectioners' (icing)
   sugar
1 quart (32 fl. oz.) softened
   vanilla ice cream

Grease and lightly flour a 15 x 10 jelly roll pan. Beat
the 4 egg yolks until thick, then beat in $^1/_3$ cup sugar
and vanilla. Beat 4 egg whites to soft peaks; slowly
add $^1/_2$ cup sugar. Beat to stiff peaks. Fold yolk
mixture into egg whites. Sift together the flour,
cocoa, baking powder, and salt. Gradually add flour
mixture to eggs, beating just until batter is smooth.
Spread in pan. Bake at 350° F for 12 to 15 minutes. Lay
out a clean towel and sprinkle with confectioners'
sugar. Turn out cake on towel. Roll up cake with
towel from narrow end of cake. Cool on rack. Unroll;
remove towel. Spread ice cream evenly over cake.
Reroll; wrap in aluminum foil. Freeze for 6 hours or
more before slicing and serving.

Most of us can remember a time when a birthday ...
brightened the world as if a second sun had risen.
                                                    —Robert Lynd

Birthday Tortoni

1 quart (32 fl. oz.) softened vanilla ice cream
¹/₂ cup (4 fl. oz.) chopped candied fruit and peels
¹/₂ cup (4 fl. oz.) raisins
2 tsp. (1 ¹/₂ Br. tsp.) almond extract
cherry halves and slivered almonds
  (or shredded coconut)

Blend fruit into ice cream. Add almond extract.
Spoon mixture into paper baking cups lining a
muffin tin. Top with cherry halves and almonds (or
coconut). Freeze until firm. Insert candle into each
cup, if desired.

Ice Cream Crunch

Fold 1 cup (8 fl. oz.) of finely crushed toffee candy or
miniature chocolate chips into 1 quart (32 fl. oz.)
softened vanilla ice cream. (You may also use a cup
of chopped nuts or crumbled chocolate cookies, or a
mixture of crunchy ingredients.) Spoon ice cream
mixture into paper baking cups lining a muffin tin.
Freeze until firm.

*The great thing about getting older is that
you don't lose all the other ages you've been.*
—Madeleine L'Engle

Chocolate Chip Pizzas

¹/₂ lb. softened butter
1 cup (8 fl. oz.) packed brown sugar
¹/₂ cup (4 fl. oz.) granulated sugar
2 eggs
1 ¹/₂ tsp. (1 Br. tsp.) vanilla extract
¹/₂ tsp. each: cinnamon, nutmeg, salt
1 ¹/₂ cups (12 fl. oz.) all-purpose flour
1 tsp. (³/₄ Br. tsp.) baking soda
2 cups (16 fl. oz.) rolled oats
1 cup (8 fl. oz.) shredded coconut
1 ¹/₄ cups (10 fl. oz.) chocolate chips

Heat oven to 350° F. Grease five 8-inch pie pans. Place
a round of wax paper in each pan; grease the paper.
Cream together butter and the sugars until fluffy.
Beat in eggs, vanilla, spices and salt. Stir in rest of
ingredients except chocolate chips. Divide dough into
5 equal parts; spread dough evenly in pans. Sprinkle
¹/₄ cup chips on each pizza. Bake 15 to 20 minutes or
until browned. Cool in pans. Turn out pizzas and
remove paper. Cut in wedges to serve.

Live your life while you have it.
Life is a splendid gift.
—Florence Nightingale

Life is a series of surprises, and
would not be worth taking or keeping
if it were not.

—Ralph Waldo Emerson

21

Fruit Pizza

Try this easy-to-make "pie" as an attractive and refreshing dessert for a summer cookout or barbecue.

one roll of refrigerated (prepackaged) sugar cookie
    dough
8 ounces softened cream cheese
confectioners' (icing) sugar
sliced kiwi fruit
one small can of mandarin oranges
sliced fresh strawberries
peach slices
bing cherry halves
seedless grape halves
pineapple tidbits

Roll out dough on floured surface. With floured hands, spread dough thinly on an ungreased pizza pie pan and bake according to package directions (usually at 350° F for about 10 minutes or until golden brown). Spread cream cheese over cookie crust and sprinkle sugar on cream cheese. Arrange fruit slices in pattern on top of cream cheese. Refrigerate before serving. Slice into wedges to serve. Refrigerate leftovers.

Those who bring sunshine to the lives of others cannot keep it from themselves.
—Sir James Barrie

Take-Along Date Bars

Here's a sweet treat and energy snack that can be carried with you outdoors while hiking, backpacking, picnicking, etc.

1 3/4 cups (14 fl. oz.) flour
1 1/4 cups (10 fl. oz.) sugar
1 cup (8 fl. oz.) whole bran cereal
1/2 cup (4 fl. oz.) vegetable oil
1/3 cup (2 2/3 fl. oz.) dark corn syrup
1 tsp. (3/4 Br. tsp.) each: salt, baking powder, cinnamon
2 eggs
1 cup (8 fl. oz.) chopped pitted dates
1/2 cup (4 fl. oz.) chopped almonds or pecans

Heat oven to 325° F. Grease and flour a 15 x 10 jelly roll pan. In a large bowl beat all ingredients except dates and nuts with an electric mixer on low speed, until just mixed. Increase speed to medium. Beat for 1 minute, continuously scraping the bowl with a rubber spatula. (Batter should be stiff.) Stir in dates and nuts with a spoon. Spread mixture in pan. Bake for 35 minutes or until inserted toothpick comes out clean. Cool in pan on a wire rack. Cut into bars with a sharp, sturdy knife and wrap individually for easy carrying or storage.

To travel hopefully is a better thing than to arrive.
—Robert Louis Stevenson

24

Here are two simple and delicious desserts to make on your barbecue or grill after the main meal while the coals are still hot.

Fruit Kabobs

Have ready chunks or cubes of peach, apple, apricot, banana, and pineapple, plus whole strawberries and large seedless grapes. Carefully thread the fruit onto skewers. Brush the fruit with melted butter and sprinkle with granulated sugar, or brush with a mixture of brown sugar, lemon juice, and orange juice. Barbecue the skewer of fruit over hot coals, turning often. Baste again. Serve when fruit is still slightly crisp and sugar has carmelized.

Angel Food Kabobs

Cut pieces of angel food cake or pound cake into 2-inch cubes. Using a fork, dip the cubes in sweetened condensed milk, then roll in flaked coconut. Spear on skewers, alternating cake with large marshmallows. Toast kabobs over hot coals, turning often, until golden brown.

How beautiful a day can be when kindness touches it.
—George Elliston

❧ THINGS TO SHARE ❧ & SHOW YOU CARE

Chocolate Muffins

$1/2$ lb. unsalted butter
4 ounces sweet baking chocolate
$1\,3/4$ cups (14 fl. oz.) sugar
1 cup (8 fl. oz.) sifted, unbleached all-purpose flour
dash of salt
$1/4$ tsp. nutmeg or mace
4 eggs
1 tsp. ($3/4$ Br. tsp.) vanilla extract
2 cups (16 fl. oz.) chopped pecans

Heat oven to 300° F. Line muffin tins with paper
baking cups. In the top of a double boiler over
simmering water, melt butter and chocolate. Mix
sugar, flour, salt, and spice in a large bowl. Stir in the
chocolate/butter mixture. Add eggs and vanilla. Mix
until batter is evenly moistened; do not overmix. Stir
in pecans. Spoon batter into cups, filling two-thirds
full. Bake for about 40 minutes or until inserted
toothpick comes out clean from center of a muffin.
Cool on racks.

It is not enough to love those
who are near and dear to us.
We must show them that we do so.
—Lord Avebury

We find rest in those we love, and we provide a
resting place in ourselves for those who love us.
—Bernard of Clairvaux

Sweetie Pies

Take time while you're working in the kitchen to make these delicious little treats for someone you love, using leftover scraps of pie crust dough.

Cinnamon Pinwheels

Gather leftover scraps of dough into a ball; roll out into a rectangle about 1/8-inch thick. Dot surface of rectangle with butter. Sprinkle with sugar and cinnamon. Roll rectangle into a long roll; seal the seams. Place on baking sheet with lip around its edge (to catch melted butter). Bake at 425° F for about 20 minutes or until golden brown. Cool, slice, and serve.

Mini Turnovers

Heat oven to 475° F. Gather leftover dough into a ball. Shape into a flattened round. Roll out to 1/8-inch thickness. Cut dough into circles; cut a small hole out of the center of half the circles. Put a dab of jelly on the whole circles, then top with the circles that have holes. Seal edges of circles together. Place on ungreased baking sheet. Bake for 8 to 10 minutes.

Work is love made visible.
—Kahlil Gibran

Banana Bread

¹/₄ lb. butter
1 cup (8 fl. oz.) sugar
2 slightly beaten eggs
3 medium-sized ripe bananas, mashed
1 cup (8 fl. oz.) sifted all-purpose flour
¹/₂ tsp. each ginger and salt
1 tsp. (³/₄ Br. tsp.) baking soda
1 cup (8 fl. oz.) whole wheat flour
¹/₃ cup (2 ²/₃ fl. oz.) hot water
¹/₂ cup (4 fl. oz.) chopped walnuts

Heat oven to 325° F. Grease a 9 x 5 loaf pan. Melt butter. Blend in sugar. Mix in eggs and bananas. Blend until smooth. Sift all-purpose flour again with salt, soda, and ginger. Stir in whole wheat flour. Add dry ingredients to banana mixture, alternating with hot water. Stir in nuts. Bake for about 60 to 70 minutes.

I know of no better way of being happy
than in making others so.
—John Greenleaf Whittier

A GIRL'S BEST FRIEND IS HER MOTHER

Like everything breathing of kindness—
Like these is the love of a friend.
—A. P. Stanley

Chocolate Strawberry Shortcake

4 cups (32 fl. oz.) fresh
strawberries
1/4 cup (2 fl. oz.) granulated
sugar
1 2/3 cups (13 1/3 fl. oz.) all-
purpose flour
1/3 cup (2 2/3 fl. oz.) unsweetened cocoa powder
1/4 cup (2 fl. oz.) granulated
sugar
1 tbsp. (3/4 Br. tbsp.) baking
powder
1/4 tsp. salt
1/2 tsp. mace
1/4 lb. cold butter, cut in
pieces
1 beaten egg
2/3 cup (5 1/3 fl. oz.) milk
1 cup (8 fl. oz.) whipping
cream
2 tbsp. (1 1/2 Br. tbsp.)
confectioners' (icing)
sugar
1/2 tsp. vanilla extract

Set aside a few strawberries for garnishing. Slice the
remaining berries; combine with 1/4 cup granulated
sugar. Let stand. Heat oven to 450° F. Combine flour,
cocoa powder, 1/4 cup granulated sugar, baking
powder, salt, and mace in a mixing bowl. Cut in butter
until mixture is crumbly. Mix egg and milk, then add
to dry mixture. Stir just enough to moisten. Spread
dough evenly in an 8-inch round pan. Bake for 15 to 18
minutes or until cake pulls away from side of pan.
Cool pan on a wire rack for 15 minutes. Turn onto a
serving plate. Beat whipping cream with confectioners' sugar until soft peaks form. Add vanilla; beat until
cream is right consistency. Spoon berries on top of
cake. Swirl whipped cream over berries. Garnish with
reserved berries and serve.

Raspberry-Sherry Trifle

Custard:
2 cups (16 fl. oz.) whole milk
4 eggs
2 tbsp. (1 ½ Br. tbsp.) sugar
½ tsp. vanilla extract

Fillings:
24 ladyfingers or strips of sponge cake
1 cup (8 fl. oz.) sherry
8 ounces raspberry jam
¾ cup (6 fl. oz.) sliced candied cherries or sliced
    strawberries
¾ cup (6 fl. oz.) toasted sliced almonds

Topping:
1 cup (8 fl. oz.) heavy cream
3 tbsp. (2 ¼ Br. tbsp.) sugar
½ tsp. almond extract

*Christmas hath a beauty
Lovelier than the world can show.*
    —Christina Rossetti

In a heavy saucepan, heat milk over low heat until very hot, but not boiling. While milk heats, beat together eggs, sugar, and vanilla in a large bowl. Pour hot milk very slowly into egg mixture, stirring constantly. Mix thoroughly; pour into saucepan. Stir over medium heat until custard is thickened. Pour into clean container; cover and chill slightly.

Tip: To keep skin from forming on custard, cut out a piece of waxed paper to fit directly onto the surface of the custard, then gently peel off paper when ready to use.

Arrange a layer of ladyfingers on the bottom and sides of a 2-quart crystal bowl. Sprinkle with half the sherry. Pour half of custard over cake. Dot with raspberry jam, half of almonds, and half of cherries. Repeat steps with a second layer, saving a few cherries for decoration. Whip the cream until soft peaks form. Beat in sugar and almond extract. Spread over surface of trifle. Pipe any remaining whipped cream through a pastry bag with a decorative tip to form a pattern on trifle. Decorate with cherry halves. Refrigerate until serving.

"But I am sure I have always thought of Christmastime ... as a good time ... and I say, God bless it!"
—Charles Dickens

IT IS A FINE SEASONING
FOR JOY TO THINK
OF THOSE WE LOVE.
·MOLIERE·

Sugar Angels

$^1/_2$ lb. softened butter
1 $^1/_2$ cups (12 fl. oz.) confectioners' (icing) sugar
1 egg
1 tsp. ($^3/_4$ Br. tsp.) vanilla extract
$^1/_2$ tsp. almond extract
2 $^1/_2$ cups (20 fl. oz.) flour
1 tsp. ($^3/_4$ Br. tsp.) baking soda
1 tsp. ($^3/_4$ Br. tsp.) cream of tartar
granulated sugar

Mix together the butter, confectioners' sugar, egg,
vanilla, and almond extract. Blend in flour, baking
soda, and cream of tartar. Cover dough. Chill 2 to 3
hours. Heat oven to 375° F. On floured surface roll out
part of dough to $^3/_{16}$-inch thickness. Keep remaining
dough chilled. Using an angel-shaped cookie cutter,
cut out cookies. Sprinkle with granulated sugar. Place
on lightly greased baking sheet. Bake 7 to 8 minutes or
until light brown on edges. Repeat process with
remaining dough.

*. . . it is good to be children sometimes,
and never better than at Christmas . . .*
—Charles Dickens

Lemon Gingerbread

Gingerbread:

2 ¼ cups (18 fl. oz.) cake flour*
⅓ cup (2 ⅔ fl. oz.) sugar
1 cup (8 fl. oz.) dark molasses
¾ cup (6 fl. oz.) hot water
¼ lb. butter
1 egg
1 tsp. (¾ Br. tsp.) each:
  baking soda, ginger,
  cinnamon
¾ tsp. salt

Lemon Glaze:

2 cups (16 fl. oz.) confection-
  ers' (icing) sugar
1 tbsp. (¾ Br. tbsp.) corn-
  starch
3 tbsp. (2 ¼ Br. tbsp.) milk
2 tbsp. (1 ½ Br. tbsp.)
  lemon juice
½ tsp. vanilla extract

Heat oven to 325° F. Grease and flour a 9 x 9 x 2 baking pan. In a large mixing bowl, blend all gingerbread ingredients for 30 seconds on slow speed, scraping the bowl constantly. Beat another 3 minutes on medium speed, scraping bowl occasionally. Pour into pan. Bake 50 minutes or until toothpick inserted in center comes out clean. Let cool in pan on wire rack for 10 minutes, then turn onto serving plate. Poke holes in top of bread with a toothpick. Mix dry ingredients of glaze. Slowly add liquids. Beat until smooth, then drizzle over gingerbread.

*Do not use self-rising flour.

Love that giveth in full store,
Aye, receives as much and more.
    —Dinah Maria Craik

MAY

THE BLESSED LIGHT BE ON YOU,
LIGHT WITHOUT & LIGHT WITHIN.
MAY THE BLESSED SUNLIGHT
SHINE ON YOU & WARM YOUR HEART
UNTIL IT GLOWS LIKE A GREAT FIRE,
SO THAT A STRANGER MAY COME
& WARM HIMSELF AT IT & ALSO
A FRIEND. MAY GOD ALWAYS
BLESS YOU, LOVE YOU, & KEEP YOU

Eggnog Cake

Cake:

2 cups (16 fl. oz.) all-purpose flour

2 tsp. (1 1/2 Br. tsp.) baking powder

1/2 tsp. nutmeg

1/4 tsp. ginger

1/2 tsp. salt

1/2 tsp. vanilla extract

1 1/2 cups (12 fl. oz.) heavy cream

4 eggs

1 1/4 cups (10 fl. oz.) sugar

Frosting:

1/4 lb. softened butter

4 1/2 cups (36 fl. oz.) confectioners' (icing) sugar

1/2 tsp. nutmeg

3 tbsp. (2 1/4 Br. tbsp.) orange juice

2 tsp. (1 1/2 Br. tsp.) grated orange peel

strips of orange peel

Heat oven to 350° F. Grease and flour three 9-inch round layer cake pans. Combine first 5 cake ingredients in mixing bowl. In second bowl beat cream and vanilla with an electric mixer on medium speed until stiff peaks form. In large mixing bowl, beat eggs and sugar at high speed for 5 minutes. Fold flour mixture and cream mixture into egg mixture until blended. Pour batter into cake pans. Stagger pans on oven racks so no pan is directly above another. Bake 20 to 25 minutes or until toothpick inserted in center comes out clean. Cool pans on wire racks for 10 minutes; remove cakes from pans. Cool for 1 hour before frosting. To make frosting, blend butter, sugar, and nutmeg. Stir in juice and grated peel. Stir until smooth and of spreading consistency. Cut each layer of cake

horizontally in half with a sharp knife. Place first
layer on cake plate, cut side up. Frost with about $\frac{1}{2}$
cup (4 fl. oz.) frosting. Repeat with next 4 layers. Place
last layer with top side up. Frost top and sides of cake.
Garnish with strips of orange peel.

Respect is what we owe; love, what we give.
—Philip James Bailey

Chocolate Pecan Pie

1 $\frac{1}{2}$ cups (12 fl. oz.) coarsely chopped pecans
6 ounces semisweet chocolate chips
1 partially baked 8-inch pie shell
$\frac{1}{2}$ cup (4 fl. oz.) light corn syrup
$\frac{1}{2}$ cup (4 fl. oz.) sugar
2 extra large eggs
4 tbsp. (3 Br. tbsp.) butter, melted and cooled

Heat oven to 325° F. Evenly distribute the nuts and
chocolate chips in the empty pie shell. Mix corn
syrup, eggs, and sugar in a bowl, then blend in the
butter. Pour the syrup mixture slowly and evenly
over the nut and chocolate chip mixture. Bake for
about 60 minutes or until firm.

The best moments of a visit are those
which again and again postpone its close.
—Jean Paul Richter

Double Chocolate Chip Cookies

2 cups (16 fl. oz.) unsifted all-purpose flour
$^1/_2$ cup (4 fl. oz.) unsweetened cocoa powder
1 tsp. ($^3/_4$ Br. tsp.) baking soda
1 tsp. ($^3/_4$ Br. tsp.) salt
$^1/_2$ lb. softened butter
1 $^1/_4$ cups (10 fl. oz.) granulated sugar
$^3/_4$ cup (6 fl. oz.) packed brown sugar
1 $^1/_2$ tsp. (1 Br. tsp.) vanilla extract
2 eggs
12 ounces semisweet chocolate chips
$^3/_4$ cup (6 fl. oz.) chopped almonds

Heat oven to 375° F. In a small mixing bowl combine
flour, cocoa, baking soda, and salt. In a large mixing
bowl combine butter, granulated sugar, brown sugar,
and vanilla. Beat until creamy. Beat in eggs. Gradually
add flour mixture. Mix well. Stir in chocolate chips
and nuts. Drop mixture in rounded teaspoonfuls
onto ungreased cookie sheet. Bake for 8 to 10 minutes
or until edges of cookies are firm. Cool for a minute,
then transfer cookies to a wire rack to continue
cooling.

Love and you shall be loved.
—Ralph Waldo Emerson

THE
PRINCESS
OF
QUITE·A·LOT

Mocha Mousse

4 ounces sweet cooking chocolate
¹/₂ cup (4 fl. oz.) light cream
2 tsp. (1 ¹/₂ Br. tsp.) instant coffee
1 tbsp. (³/₄ Br. tbsp.) sugar
2 separated eggs
¹/₂ tsp. vanilla extract
¹/₄ cup (2 fl. oz.) sugar

In a medium saucepan heat chocolate, cream, coffee, and 1 tbsp. sugar, stirring constantly until chocolate melts and mixture is smooth. Remove from heat. Beat the egg yolks slightly. Slowly stir chocolate mixture into yolks. Add vanilla. Beat egg whites until foamy. Beat in rest of sugar, a little at a time, until stiff peaks form. Fold egg white mixture into chocolate mixture. Pour into small serving cups. Chill for at least 30 minutes before serving.

Love comforteth like sunshine after rain.
—William Shakespeare

Sour Cream Cheesecake

1 1/4 cups (10 fl. oz.) graham
    cracker (digestive
    biscuit) crumbs
2 tbsp. (1 1/2 Br. tbsp.) sugar
3 tbsp. (2 1/4 Br. tbsp.)
    melted butter
two 8-ounce pkgs. softened
    cream cheese
one 3-oz. pkg. softened
    cream cheese
1 cup (8 fl. oz.) sugar
2 tsp. (1 1/2 Br. tsp.) grated
    lemon peel

1/4 tsp. vanilla extract
3 eggs
1 cup (8 fl. oz.) sour
    cream
2 tbsp. (1 1/2 Br. tbsp.)
    confectioners' (icing)
    sugar
1 tsp. (3/4 Br. tsp.) vanilla
    extract
sliced strawberries for
    garnishing

Heat oven to 350° F. Stir together crumbs and 2 tbsp.
sugar. Blend in butter thoroughly. Press crumb
mixture in bottom of 9-inch springform (loose
bottom) pan. Bake for 10 minutes and cool. Turn
heat down to 300° F. Beat cream cheese in a large
bowl with an electric mixer. Slowly beat in sugar
until fluffy. Add vanilla and lemon peel. Beat in eggs,
one at a time. Pour mixture over crust. Bake until
center is firm (about 1 hour). Cool to room temperature. Combine sour cream, confectioners' sugar and
vanilla, then spread mixture on cheesecake. Garnish
top with strawberries. Chill at least 4 hours. Before
removing side of pan, loosen cheesecake with a knife.

Fudge Brownies

4 ounces unsweetened chocolate
$^1/_2$ lb. butter
2 cups (16 fl. oz.) sugar
3 beaten eggs
1 tsp. ($^3/_4$ Br. tsp.) vanilla extract
1 cup (8 fl. oz.) chopped pecans
1 cup (8 fl. oz.) sifted flour
$^1/_4$ tsp. salt

Heat oven to 350° F. Grease and flour a 9-inch square
baking pan. Melt chocolate and butter over low heat.
Remove from heat. Add sugar, eggs, and vanilla. Mix
well. Stir in nuts. Sift flour and salt together. Add
them to liquid mixture, mixing thoroughly. Pour into
prepared pan. Bake for 45 to 50 minutes. Cool com-
pletely before cutting into squares.

The happiness of life is made up of minute fractions ...
a kiss or smile, a kind look, a heartfelt compliment ...
—Samuel Taylor Coleridge

Orange-Chocolate Truffles

5 ounces unsweetened chocolate
8 ounces softened cream cheese
1 lb. confectioners' (icing) sugar
1 tsp. (³/₄ Br. tsp.) orange extract or orange liqueur
1 tsp. (³/₄ Br. tsp.) grated orange zest
cocoa powder or confectioners' (icing) sugar

Melt chocolate over hot water in double boiler.
Remove from heat. Blend cream cheese and sugar in a
mixing bowl. Add the melted chocolate, the orange
flavoring, and orange zest. Mix well. Refrigerate until
firm. Shape into balls. Roll in cocoa powder or confectioners' sugar. Store in a tightly covered container in
the refrigerator.

Love is the reward of love.
—Johann von Schiller

46

Mary Engelbreit is an internationally recognized artist and designer, whose work combines warmth, wit, nostalgia, and a unique style. Born and raised in a St. Louis, Missouri suburb, her artistic talent surfaced early. Though mostly self-taught, she attended summer art classes as a teenager. After several years working as a commercial illustrator, Mary signed with Portal Publications, where she established a national reputation. She started her own greeting card company, which she eventually sold to Sunrise Publications. Since 1982 she has developed a strong licensing program. Her designs appear on a wide variety of products, including tins, mugs, plates, Christmas ornaments, picture frames, clothing, and textiles. Mary still lives and works in St. Louis with her husband and two young sons.